Acknowledgments:

Mom- I know you will never read this, but hey I said I would say thank you for having sex and birthing me.

Ronni L.- Thank you for all your support and love of Draven and Poppet. You truly are amazing.

Kari- You are a wonderful person. Thank you for loving my characters and supporting my writing.

Kayla P.- You are always on board to read whatever I'm writing. Thank you for helping me.

Deana W.- Thank you for being apart of the process and being an alpha reader. I'm sorry this book grossed you out.

Christina R.- You are amazing my friend. Thank you for sharing my work and lifting my spirits.

Alpha and ARC readers- thank you for taking time to read my book. It means so much to me to have such a wonderful team. There isn't enough words to say how grateful I am.

1

Dear Reader,

Thank you to everyone who read Funhouse and loved Draven and Poppet! I'm glad you took a chance on my Killer Klowns! Don't expect the same thing from Carousel however, this book takes the naughtiness of Funhouse to extremes. No , seriously. This novella has all the triggers, I mean like all of them or to some of you a shopping list of good sexy funtimes. But in case you want a peekaboo list of what you might encounter in this book trigger wise here it goes:

Trigger warnings: Face smacking, Spitting, golden showers (water play), Assault, Attempted rape, blood, blood play, branding, Drugs (marijuana usage), Gore, Murder, Profanity, Sexuality explicit scenes, Torture, violence, fat phobic slur (but the guy is an asshole), dismantling a body, knife play, fisting, snowballing, cum swapping

Tropes: Double penetration, double vagina penetration, MMF, inanimate object usage in sex, coulrophilia, masks, handcuffs, BDSM, exhabition, voyeurism, MM scenes, threesomes, FM scenes, usage of pet names, Domme/sub/sub, Dom/sub/sub, anal play,

LIKE I'M GIVING YOU a chance to close this book and stop reading. Because it gets very naughty. Like you are gonna be like WTF did I just read? So, continue at your own risk.

Well, then If you want to email me you can do that at jamiespicerauthor@gmail.com

Happy Reading,

Jamie XOXO

.

Music Playlist:

1. Dirty- Christina Aguilera
2. I'm a slave 4 U- Brittany Spears
3. Carousel- Melanie Martinez
4. My love is like Woah- Mya
5. Get UR freak on- Missy Elliot
6. My neck, my back- Khia
7. S&M - Rihanna
8. I spit on your Grave-Zand
9. Trip Switch- Nothing but Thieves
10. Wait and Bleed- Slipknot
11. Vertigo- Derik Fein

Dedication:

To all the bad girls who like bad boys. The ladies who like to take charge, and the ones who love them. The freaks, outcasts, and the carnies.

This is

Your last chance

To close the book.

Okay, I warned you!

Have fun!

You're F*cked- Mehki

"That's it, baby, no one can suck my cock like you." I look down into ocean eyes, as they peer up at me, devouring my praises like they are Jesus at the last supper, "You can take me deeper, I know you can." I thrust hard grabbing the back of my dick suckers blonde head and smirk when I hear them gag.

I grasp the hair of the person kneeling in front of me, my dick slides out of their mouth. My grasp tight, I pull them up from the ground, facing me, then spin them around to face the wall.

"Bend over slut, Daddy's going to make you feel good." I push down on their head and grab their hair pulling it back toward me, I lick up the side of their face tasting the saltiness of the sweat they are perspiring then shove it back down.

I spit a good amount of sputum in my hand and fist my hard cock, "This might hurt just a little." I slide my dick between their ass cheeks, and without a warning or time to prepare I buck my hips slipping my dick into their tight ass hole.

"Oh, God," they groan, as I begin to fuck them without abandon. I know the lack of lube is causing them pain, but I don't care.

I spit on my cock and watch as my saliva lubricates their asshole, when I hear moaning I know that the pain of me taking them roughly is easing and they are now enjoying this just as much as I am.

"Fuck, you are so tight around me. Tell Daddy you love his cock." I pull their sweaty locks of golden hair forcing their head to turn looking deep into my eyes.

"I love your cock daddy." their eyes are heated with fire. "Now make me come."

"Well, well, well. What the hell did I just walk into?" A woman's voice comes from the doorway. I turn around and peek over my shoulder, still fucking the person beneath me. The tall shapely figure begins to sway towards me.

"Wait in line bitch," I mutter, as my eyes roll back when my orgasm intensifies. I pull out and spray my jizz all over their back. "Give me like fifteen minutes and I will be ready for you." I call over my shoulder as I start stuffing my flaccid dick into my jeans.

The woman starts laughing, as if I'm joking, and before I know it she takes a wooden baseball bat to the back of my knees causing me to hit the hard concrete floor.

"You will show me respect when you talk to me. Do you understand?" I glare up at her and notice the mask she is wearing. "Say yes, Mistress Rogue. "

I gaze at the person I just fucked, they are now standing watching the woman with amazement, before I know it the woman slaps me as hard as she can, busting my lip in the process. When I open my mouth to scream, she sticks her fingers into my mouth pulling my lower jaw down, blood begins pouring from my lip. She looks me in the eyes as she expectorates into my mouth, then smiles before removing her fingers from my lips.

"Now, say yes, Mistress Rogue." She looks down at me waiting to see what I will do.

I grin at the gorgeous woman and do exactly what she says. "Yes, Mistress Rogue."

"Good boy, Pet." She pats my head as if I were a puppy. She gathers some of the blood that is dripping from my lip and looks at it as if she is solving a mystery, and then draws something on my forehead with it.

As the woman turns, the staccato beat of her high heels fills the storage area, her hips swaying from side to side with each confident step, commanding the attention of all those around her.

"Holy fuck! Who was that?" Jordan looks at me and I turn to look over at the door where Mistress Rogue exited from. "What the fuck does A mean?"

"A? I have no fucking clue, but I want her," I say, taking some paper towels off a roll that's sitting on a box. "Turn around baby and I will clean you up."

"I want her too, Mehki," Jordan says, turning around and lifting his shirt so I can wipe the cum off his back.

When he is clean, he turns around and grabs the paper towel and begins to wipe at the spot where the woman wiped my blood on my forehead, "What is it? What are you wiping from my forehead, Jordan?"

"The letter A." Jordan throws the paper towel in the trash. "What the fuck just happened? Why the letter A?"

Incognito- Ann

I ALWAYS SUSPECTED those two were fucking. I walk into my traveling camper, that they forced me to live in during the summer months and remove my mask and shoes. Those fuckwads are so unaware of everyone and everything, they will never guess the shy, blonde girl who runs the carousel is the person that just made Mehki, the guy that everyone knows as the carnival prick, her bitch. I place the mask in my closet along with my wooden Louisville Slugger. I can't risk anyone realizing it is me. I take off the high heels and step out of the dress and stockings I had been wearing and change into a big oversized tee shirt and a pair of nineties cartoon sleeping pants.

I place my long, dirty blonde hair up into a ponytail and put on my glasses, back to being my meek and mild self. I snatch a soda from the refrigerator and take a seat on the small built-in couch that is uncomfortable as fuck. I turn on some old Ren and Stimpy cartoons and light what is left of a joint I had smoked earlier in the day.

I was happy when I found out that there was going to be a carnival coming to town for the whole summer and that they needed on-site help. I never heard of this before, but since the recent floods and the community needing some positivity, the mayor must have worked out some kind of deal with the owner. I had nothing better to do during my summer break. I didn't have classes until the end of August so I figured I would give this a try. I have been working and living on the property for almost a month now and those two guys never even looked in my direction, let alone knew who I was.

Last year, one of the carnivals that came into town had a carnie kidnap two people and killed another crazy bitch that was working with her. Rumor has it that Poppet the Killer Klown and Draven from the funhouse were the ones that were kidnapped, something about his crazy ex-girlfriend getting with her crazy ex-girlfriend. It all gets pretty much hazy after that fact. I swear I have never seen two psychopaths in love until I saw them. They complete each other like peanut butter and chocolate.

I don't talk to anyone here, they all seem to look at me differently like I am not one of them. The thing is I am. I am just as much an outsider, a freak, someone society wouldn't understand. I just don't look the part on most days. When you look at me, you would never think that this hillbilly country girl used to be a member of a pretentious sex club and that I was the femme dom that everyone came to get punished by. I take the last hit of the joint and put it in the ashtray. I hold in the smoke for a few seconds then blow it out. The overwhelming feeling of peace hits me and soon my eyes flutter asleep.

Jealousy Is A Bitch- Jordan

EVER SINCE THE OTHER day when that Rogue chick caught us fucking and interrupted me getting fucked like a jackhammer, Mehki has become obsessed. I get it, that woman was fucking amazing with her long shapely legs, her blonde hair, and the way she had Mehki on his knees like a little bitch, it was fucking hot.

However, he seems consumed by her, he wakes up talking about wanting to find her and goes to bed fucking me and wishing it were her. I know it sounds like I am being a little whiney cunt, but I think I may have lost him to a woman we don't even know, the worst thing about it is, I am not just fucking Mehki, I care about him. So, even though I too am intrigued by the masked woman known only as Rogue, I am intimidated by her.

Usually, when Mehki and I are fucking he is always the dominant, but lately, he is wanting me to dominate him. I am submissive by nature, and I don't enjoy making him do the things he asks of me.

"Damn it Jor, just do it. I promise you I will enjoy it." Mehki is naked standing before me and holding a plastic clothes hanger he got from the closet.

"You want me to beat you with this hanger? Are you sure?" Mehki is the one that is rough with me and I like it. Usually, he takes what he wants from me, but now he wants me to take control and I am not good at it.

He lowers himself down in front of me and takes my cock into his hand, I am average size, he takes me in his mouth, my whole dick being swallowed by him. I whimper as he grabs my balls and begins to play with them. I snatch him by the hair, holding his head still as I start pumping my dick in and out of him. His dark eyes look up at me and I pull myself out of his mouth before he can react, I smack him as hard as I can. A grunt leaves him and he grins up at me.

"You know what I want, baby, give it to me." Mehki stands up at me and hands me the clothes hanger he picked up off the floor that he dropped when he began sucking my dick.

I pick up the hanger and close my eyes, I swing the hanger back and hit him in his torso hard, then his arms and his legs. I can see the blaze of heat in his eyes, he is turned on and pissed off. I hold my arm back to hit him again, and he grabs my arm, takes the hanger from my hand, and throws it on the floor. He grabs me by my throat and throws me against the wall. I hit the wall with a thud and he crashes his mouth to mine, his teeth graze my lip, cutting it, and blood trickles down. He takes his tongue and licks up the blood before he kisses me again. I can taste the metallic from the blood in my mouth. He forces me down and grabs his dick.

"Open your mouth, Jordan," he commands, as he strokes his cock. He stares down at me, and when I open wide he pisses in my mouth his urine flowing all over my face and down my neck, covering me in his fluids.

When he has emptied his bladder on me, his ultimate form of marking, I stand up and bend over. I am ready for him. He grabs some lube and rubs it on himself. The oily substance shines on his hard cock, he grabs my hips, puts his dick up to my ass, and thrusts into me. He takes me hard and fast. I jack myself off and we cum at the same time. I orgasm filling my hand full of my jizz, and when he pulls away from inside me, I turn around and smear my cum all over his face.

"Bet that Rogue bitch can't do that for you!" I hiss, treading into the bathroom leaving him standing there drenched in the results of our sex.

Her- Mehki

I CAN'T GET THE GIRL off my mind, and I know that Jordan notices the change in me. I try not to let it affect our relationship, but I have become obsessed with Rogue. I look for her everywhere, the stores nearby in the small town in Kentucky we are currently staying for the summer, every time a blonde walks into the fun house haunt, every person who walks by in the carnival, but she is nowhere to be found. I am sure Rogue doesn't carry around a baseball bat or wear a mask everywhere she goes, but come on I am sure to find someone similar to her in some way.

Obsessed. That is the only word that describes it. I want her and I will not give up until she is mine, ours, but mostly mine. I go to bed with her on my mind, when I fuck Jordan, she is on my mind, and when I get up in the morning she is there too. Hell even when I am eating I think about the way she had spit into my mouth and the slap that stunned the fuck out of me. I have never had a woman that could make me feel the way she does, and I fucking love it.

It's a hot and humid summer night, the fun house is busy with customers. I wipe the sweat from my brow and listen as Draven and his chick Poppet scare the first round of patrons. The noises of the frightened crowd make me laugh, this is like a high you get from a drug, but better. Adrenaline runs through me as I hide behind a wall with my chainsaw, it is real, but the chain isn't on it. Whenever a person goes around the corner I jump out with my chainsaw and go at them and run them to where Jordan comes out with a fake ax. The looks of pure terror on the faces of the people who visit are better than ice cream.

The carnival starts winding down at midnight every night. Once the crowd leaves we are free to do what we want, usually we all just go back to our campers and rest. A few hang out by a bonfire and drink, others go to nearby towns and drink or whatever they do in the bumfucked hills of Kentucky. Jordan and I go home to our camper. We are tired and covered in sweat. The fun house has no cooling so we always roast in the metal tuna can. We decide to take a shower, never expecting who was waiting for us when we got out.

Do as I say and I won't hurt you- Rogue

THE CAROUSEL WAS SLOW tonight, mostly adults and teenagers came during the week. So, I was bored as fuck and glad when the boss said I could close up the carousel early. I ran to my little camper, took a nice hot shower, dried myself well, and grabbed the suit that I ordered online from my closet. The black catsuit was amazing and latex. I had owned a few latex items in the past, but this was a thing of beauty. I covered myself with baby powder and rolled the catsuit down making sure to use my hand to help glide it up and on. Once the outfit is in place, I take shine spray lubricant and put it all over me. The black elastomer suit shines like it is wet and I love the way it hugs my body, showing all my curves and my ample breasts. I leave my black hair down and use a straightener to straighten it. I think heels work best with this outfit, so I slip them on and grab a masquerade mask. It is black and lacey, with a feather decorating it. It only covers half of my face, from my nose down I am exposed. I put on a bright red lipstick and then look in the mirror. Excellent. Before I head out the door, I grab my baseball bat. You never know when it will come in handy.

Water can be heard running as I step up to the little red camper in which the guys live. I try the door handle but the door is locked. I feel around the door facing and find a key hidden at the top. Typical silly boys, can't even hide a key right. I shake my head as I let myself into the camper of Mehki and Jordan. There are noises coming from the bathroom, voices, water splashing around, and low music playing. I look around the tiny room that makes up a living room and a small kitchenette. It is surprisingly clean, some collectable toys are on a shelf along with some other whatnots. I creep through the short hallway and find their bedroom at the other end of the hall. It's a big queen size bed with overhead cabinets. Very small, but cozy. I take a seat at the foot of the bed and wait for the guys to come out of the teeny bathroom.

A few minutes later a blonde-haired Jordan comes out, dripping water from his unbelievably sexy body, a towel is hanging around his hips and I have to admit, I am curious to see what is behind it.

"Holy fuck." Jordan glares at me as he notices who it is that has entered his domain. "What are you doing here?"

"Who are you talking to babe?" Mehki trudges into the tiny bedroom behind him and stops abruptly.

"Me." I stand up and flash the nearly naked guy a huge smile, I throw the key up in the air and catch it. "He was talking to me. Looks like you fellas need to hide your hide-a-key better."

"I asked you a question." Jordan gives me a look of disdain and secretly, I love it. It means I got to at least one of them the other day.

"I don't answer to anyone Pup. They answer to me." I glance at Mehki who is staring at me like he is a starving man and I am a t-bone steak, "You boys up to play tonight?"

"Yes," Mehki says, quickly. While a no, immediately escapes from Jordan's lips.

"Come on Pup, I promise you will enjoy it. Let's play do as Mistress Rogue says, and she won't hurt you." I hold up my bat, and wrap my hand around it, moving it up and down as if it were a cock and I was jacking it off. "You know you want to play," I purr.

"I am not your Pup, bitch stop calling me that." Jordan spits through clenched teeth.

My baseball bat swings out and clips his thigh. "I said you are going to respect me. I am not bitch, you will refer to me as Mistress Rogue, Pup." I hold out the baseball bat to his chest, he grabs his leg and Mehki smiles an evil grin as if he is enjoying every second of this encounter.

"I will do anything you say, Jordan will too." Mehki looks at Jordan with a raised eyebrow. "Tell her Jordan, tell Mistress Rogue you will do as she says like a good boy."

The glare that Jordan gives Mehki is hot enough to burn. "I will do as you say Mistress Rogue." Jordan peers at me with a defiant glare.

"That's better Pup." I reach my hand to his chest and run my hand up to his shoulder where I put my weight on one end and push him down. "Suck Mehki's dick, I'm going to watch."

"Mehki, you are to place your hands behind your head. You are not to make a sound. You are not to move. If you do indeed make a move or a sound comes from you, you will be punished. Do you understand?" Mehki nods his head and I hold up my bat to him. "Say yes, Mistress Rogue."

"Yes, Mistress Rogue." A smirk forms on my face and I notice a glint in his eye, he likes being punished, I can tell. "If for any reason, you want to stop playing, the code word is arrêter. It means stop in french, repeat after me, arrêter. You too, Jordan." They both repeat the word back to me and then I nod my head. "Begin."

Jordan fists Mehki's already hard cock in his hands, his hands sliding up and down his shaft, when precum forms at the tip, Jordan sticks out his tongue and licks it off. A small moan comes from Mehki and I take my place on the end of the bed like the queen I am and watch the show before me. Mehki will be punished for the sound he gave, but for now, I am enjoying watching Jordan's mouth wrapped around his boyfriend's dick. Jordan's golden mane of hair flows down over his naked back, and this has to be one of the most erotic, beautiful, and sensual things I have ever experienced.

Jordan moves his hand and cups Mehki's ball sac as he begins to massage them, his head bobs up and down, taking the length of him. Mehki bites his lips trying to keep the noises of his pleasure from coming out. I can feel my wetness between my legs, I almost wish I had chosen something different to wear so I could please myself while forcing them to please each other. When I see that Mehki is obviously on the edge of coming. I stand up and walk over to Jordan, I wind my hand into his long hair and pull his back, causing Mehki's cock to slip from his lips with a loud popping noise.

"What the fuck!" Mehki yells, his dark eyes meet mine. "I was just about to cum."

"Yes, I know this. That is your punishment for disobeying me. You don't get to cum." I move closer to him and get into his face. I grab his cock that is still hard. I run my thumb over the tip and then yank it forcefully. " And that is for speaking to me the way you just did. I am in control here Pet, and you two better not forget it."

I draw my hand back and slap him across his face, but he doesn't even flinch. He is getting off on it. I can tell by the heated look in his eye. "Come here Pup," I pat my leg and Jordan looks up at me like a wounded animal, but moves to where I am.

I bend down to his level, and grab his chin with my hand, lifting his face to peer into my eyes. "Pup, you want to come, don't you? You want my Pet to make you feel good?" Jordan shakes his head yes.

"Stand up and go lay on the bed and wait for Mehki." I take his hand and help him up off his knees. Jordan, being the natural submissive that he is doing exactly as I say, laying flat on his back without saying a word.

I move in front of Mehki and grab him by his cock, making him follow along behind me as I move to the side of the bed leaving him in front of Jordan. They make eye contact with each other and wait for my instruction.

Yes, Mistress Rogue- Mehki

"I AM ASSUMING Y'ALL just raw dog it, am I right?" Mistress Rogue says, as she starts opening drawers and finally reaches our toy drawer.

She pulls out a bottle of lube, and other things, but hands the lube to me. "You need to lube up Pet, he is going to need it."

I flip the top of the bottle of lubricant and squeeze some on my hand and start to wrap it around Jordan's cock, when Rogue hands me her baseball bat.

"What do you want me to do with that?" My eyebrow raises and a sickening smile crosses her lips.

"I want you to fuck him with it, of course you need to get him ready for it. Then you are going to lube it up really well and you are going to stick it in his ass." I look down at Jordan and a weary expression comes across his face.

"You remember the safe word right?" Jordan shakes his head and looks up at Rogue.

"You need to use your words Pup. Pet and I aren't mind readers, we need to know that you want this, you do, don't you? You like pleasing Pet, you want to make him happy?" She looks down at Jordan and takes some of his hair and runs her fingers through it.

"Fuck me with the baseball bat Mehki, I want it." Jordan's eyes never leave Rogue's. Rogue bends down and kisses Jordan's lips gently.

"He will make you feel amazing, Pet." His gaze leaves Rogue's and meets mine. I lube up my cock and stick it to his entrance and then force myself inside him.

I feel Rogue's eyes on mine as she watches me fuck Jordan, I know she is enjoying herself, her nipples are peaking out very visible with the tight as fuck rubber suit she has on. I lick my lips as I drive into him harder and faster and then I rip myself out of him and place the baseball bat to his ass, a groan comes to him as I push it in. We have used toys before but nothing to the circumference of the baseball bat, this is new for both of us. I can feel the ball bat pass through the ring of muscle and I ease it in and out of him.

"Deeper!" Rogue demands, as I ease the slick wooden instrument into his tight ass hole.

"God, Pup you are doing so well," Rogue coos to Jordan. He looks up at her and reaches for her hand.

She lets him take it, and when he brings her fingers to his mouth, he kisses them, slowly skims down his chest, along his stomach, to his hard member, where she wraps her hand around him. She begins to jack him off as I fuck him with the baseball bat. I am so enthralled by them, it's fucking sexy watching her small hand on his thick cock, pumping away, and when she leans over and runs her tongue from the hilt to the tip, I feel a pang of jealousy.

Her sapphire eyes peer up at me, as she puts his tip in her mouth. "What about me? When are you going to suck my cock?"

Rogue smirks and looks up at me. "When you are a good boy like Pup, here."

With only a few thrust into her mouth, she pulls away as he comes all over himself. "Pull out the baseball bat Pet and lick the jizz off from Pup."

"Fuck you, bitch. I am not licking anything, you clean him up. You are the one that made him come." I throw the bat down on the bed and start to walk away when the bat catches me between the legs and causes instant pain. I double over hitting the floor grabbing my crotch.

"Don't you ever think it is okay to talk to me like that again." Rogue grabs me by the hair and pulls me over to where Jordan lays on the bed. " I said to lick Pup clean, fucking do it, you cum dumpster."

She has my hair wrapped around her fingers, and places my head between Jordan's legs. I swear for such a small statured woman she is fucking strong. I climb up on my knees and look up at the masked woman who has invaded my home, made me and Jordan her bitch and smile. "Yes, Mistress Rogue," I obey, leaning over and begin to lick my boyfriend's jizz off, making sure to clean it up for Mistress Rogue.

Gone- Jordan

ONCE ROGUE MADE SURE that Mehki got every drop of cum off of me, she helps me sit up, Kisses my forehead, turns to Mehki and kisses him. She takes a knife she got from our bedside table and takes my hand in hers. She glides the knife over my palm, making droplets of blood appear. She places her finger in the substance, and brings it up to my forehead where she draws what I am sure is the letter A. Then she removes her bat from the bed, and walks out of the camper. There was no goodbye, we didn't get to fuck her, she just walked out, without saying anything. I got to say, she was right. I did feel good, a little sore, but nothing I couldn't handle, and the feel of her lips on my cock was magical. I know that Mehki was jealous that she touched me and not him, but I think she did that on purpose, as punishment for his disobedient behavior. I think I have changed my mind about Mistress Rogue, I think we both need her. We need to find out who our masked femme domme is before we both lose our fucking minds.

After she left, Mehki kissed me deeply and hungrily. I swear I think it was only because he was hoping my lips still tasted like hers. That by kissing me, it was like he kissed her too. Secretly, I was happy that she kissed me first, that she had me in her mouth before Mehki. It in a strange way made me special, just like how she wanted to make sure I felt good. I was her Pup. Now, I understand the nickname. She cares about me, in a roundabout way and wants to take care of me.

Now, Mehki isn't the only one obsessed, I am, too. I looked for Mistress Rogue in every blonde-haired, blue-eyed young woman that I could find. I did notice a beautiful, young lady over by the carousel earlier. She looked about the same age as our Mistress seemed to be, but this girl wore glasses and seemed shy. Mistress Rogue, is far from shy.

"Did you find her?" Mehki asks, as soon as he has a chance.

The carnival is busy tonight, people of all ages coming into the funhouse. We haven't had our break yet and to be honest, I really needed

Mehki's dick right now. Thinking about how she had him fuck me with a baseball bat all day has me hard as a motherfucking rock. Never in a million years would I think being fucked by a bat of all objects could have been so hot. The best thing though is when she sucked my cock, her warm mouth and juicy lips were made just right for cock sucking.

Mehki shoves me into a storage closet. I immediately unbutton my jeans and pull them down, my boxers get removed next and I turn around and face the wall. I bend down, giving him easy access, as I feel the liquid drip down my ass. Mehki grabs my hips and the next thing I know I feel him invade me, his cock filling me in the most delightful way. He thrusts in and out of me, fast and hard. *God, I love it when he takes me like this.* A moan slips from my lips as he smacks my ass. I love the sting, somehow when he spanks me, the sting lingers making my orgasm more intense. I feel him as he reaches his climax, his cum comes out of me and drips down my thighs. I pull up my boxers and my pants and button them back up. He wraps his hand around my neck and pulls me to him, his grip tight, just the way I like it, he kisses my lips gently then lets go.

"We will find her babe, no worries." I turn around to exit the small room when I feel him hit me on my ass once more. God I am gone for him.

Fuck Me- Ann/ Mistress Rogue

I NOTICED JORDAN LOOKING at me earlier. I don't think he recognized me as Mistress Rogue, but his eyes watched over me for at least a few minutes. I look considerably different as Mistress Rogue, then every day Ann. The kids, lovers, and old people have been frequent all evening. I cannot wait until the clock strikes midnight and I can turn into Mistress Rogue-erella.

I LOVE THE QUIET, THE faint sounds of voices, the way this place goes from noisy to almost silent after the patrons leave. The games are closed, the rides shut down, the lights dimmed. There is a peacefulness that washes over me as I make my way to the camper where I abide.

The key I keep on a bracelet around my wrist unlocks the door to my summer home. I step inside and the faint smell of marijuana, bleach, and body spray affronts my nostrils. I need to air out this place and open a window when I smoke weed for sure. I close and lock the door behind me as I make my way through the slim hallway to the closet bathroom and turn on the water. I strip off my clothes, remove my glasses and step under the already heated water. God, I loved the feel of getting clean. Showers, baths, hell even swimming pools are amazing. I wash my hair in coconut fragrant shampoo and conditioner, Shave my legs, my pits, and my pussy leaving a triangle shape just above my vagina. I always liked being creative with my decorating of the punani. I think it is time to pay my boys a visit.

Tonight there will be no latex suit, no high heels. I am wearing a checkered schoolgirl short-skirt, no panties, a white crop top shirt with no bra, and a pair of black vans. I put my hair up in pigtails, curling them and of course a red mask similar to the one I wore the other night, except this one is red and lacey. I put on winged liner and my signature red lipstick, snatch my baseball bat from the closet, grab a knife I keep for self-defense and exit my camper. Time for me to get some play with my Pet and Pup. I lock my door and ease my way to where my boys are staying.

THERE IS NOISE FROM a television playing as I walk up to the door. It is locked, so I use the key I still had from the other night and let myself in.

"Hello boys, have you been good today?" I ask, stepping into the camper, shocking them both as they were ready to attack whoever had entered their domain without permission.

"Yes, Mistress Rogue." My boys say in unison as I close the door behind me and lock it.

"I think tonight we will have some fun. Doesn't that sound nice, Pup?" I look at the blonde that is staring me down with amusement on his face.

"Yes, Mistress Rogue," he agrees, as he gets instantly on his knees and crawls to my side. When he reaches me I bend down, kiss the top of his head and pat him like a puppy, "Good job, Pup. You are such a good boy for me."

He sits back on his haunches and looks up at me, enjoying the praise that I give him, soaking it up like a dry sponge when you get it near water. I like the eagerness in his blue eyes and how well he obeys me. Mehki on the other hand looks defiant and has his arms across his chest, waiting for his praise.

"What about you Pet? Have you been naughty or nice." I hold my bat at him, pointing at him with the end. A smirk forms on his handsome face as he steps closer to me.

He looks down at me and whispers, "naughty."

I tsk at him and shake my head, "That is too bad Pet, I was hoping that you would get a treat tonight, but instead you get to sit over there in the chair and watch instead."

"Make me." A growl comes from Mehki's clenched teeth as he steps closer to me.

I smile and walk over to the chair, Pup stays where I left him watching the scene in front of him. I pull the chair to the middle of the room, and go to where Mehki is standing. I take my baseball bat and swing it at the back of his knees causing them to buckle. His knees hitting the floor with a thump. He looks at me with pure defiance in his eyes. I sway over to him, run my fingers through his black hair and shift his head to look me in the eyes. When I do, a grin comes across his face and I know he is enjoying this just as much as I. I tangle my fingers in his locks and begin to pull him towards the chair, he resists me a little but eventually, he gives in and begins to crawl the remainder of the way.

"I want you to kneel like that, sit back on your haunches like Pup, hands on your knees, palms up, you are to keep your eyes on me at all times. Do you understand, Pet?" I say, looking him in his eyes. When I get no response, I haul my hand back and slap him across his jaw. An angered expression flashes on his face before me. "Say yes, Mistress Rogue."

He situates himself like I said his eyes, following mine as I take a seat on the chair in front of him.

"Yes, Mistress Rogue," he finally says, as I place my baseball bat against his dick like I'm going to hit him there.

I whistle and on command Jordan crawls to me and sits before me. I spread my legs and let him have a good look at my bare pussy. I stick my fingers inside of me, both men watching with anxiousness, wanting to join in.

"Do you want to taste Pup? I have been picturing you between my legs all day." Jordan nods his head. "Make me cum, Pup."

He crawls directly to me, places his hands on my thighs to spread me wide and flattens his tongue as he licks me from asshole to clit. The feeling of his tongue lashing at me feels amazing, I can tell he hasn't had much experience with eating pussy, but that is about to change.

"Pup, I want you to insert a finger into me, then another and I want you to fuck me with them. I want you to move them in an upward position like you are summoning a genie, you will feel a ridged place inside of me. When you feel that place, I want you to put your mouth on my clit and I want you to suck on me, like you do Pet. Do you understand?" I show him with my hand what I want him to do and he again nods his head.

"I want to make you feel so good, Mistress Rogue." He sticks his fingers in me and motions like I explained. I push his head into me and he takes my clit into his mouth and begins to suck me off as he finger fucks me.

The whole time Mehki is looking me in my eyes and I can tell he is dying to join in, but he is staying right where he is, for that he may just get a reward. When I tighten around Jordan's fingers and I am about to cum, I tell him to bite my clit hard and when he does. I see stars, I grab his head and push him into me so I can ride out my orgasm. When he holds his head up a grin is on his face and he knows he did a good job.

"You did so well, Pup. I am so proud of you. Since you are such a good boy, you get to tell me what you want to happen next," I say, sitting up and kissing Jordan's lips gently, tasting myself on them.

Thank You, Jordan-Mehki

"I WANT YOU TO PLEASURE Mehki as I touch myself and watch," Jordan says, looking up at the masked bombshell who seems to make it into our camper every other night to have her way with us.

"How would you like me to pleasure him, Pup? What do you want me to do?" She places her hand under his chin and raises his head to look her in the eyes.

"I want to watch you suck his cock," Jordan says loudly with a glint in his eyes.

"Are you sure that is what you want Pup? You don't want me to suck you off instead?" She asks him as she strokes his hair.

"Yes, Mistress Rogue. I want you to suck his cock and I want to watch. I also want permission to jack off while you do." She nods her head and looks over at me.

"Come here Pet. It seems like your boy toy wants you to have a good night tonight." I crawl to her and she holds out her hand to help me stand.

I am already hard from watching Jordan eat her pussy and when she shoves my pants down and begins fisting my cock I am elated. She brings her tongue and licks the tip, circling it with her tongue. It takes everything in me to keep from grabbing her hair and forcing myself down her throat. But when she does finally pull me into her warm, waiting mouth it is like heaven. She moves her head, massaging my balls with one hand. I love the way she is making me feel. I notice Jordan has his cock out and is already touching himself off to the rhythm in which Mistress Rogue is bobbing her head. I feel the tightening in my stomach as I cum in her mouth and before I know it she pops her mouth off of me, full of my jizz and goes to Jordan, using her hand to open his lips and spits my jizz into his waiting mouth , where he drinks me down.

"Now, get down on your knees and crawl to Pup and finish him off, Pet." She takes her seat back and watches as I once again get back on my knees and crawl to my boyfriend where I take his cock into my mouth and get him off drinking his jizz down just like he had mine.

Once we are finished, Mistress Rogue stands up, walks to us, a shiny object showing in her hand. She pulls my hair and my head goes back. Mistress Rogue is looking me in the eyes as she takes a knife and runs it across the flesh of my cheek. She gathers some on her finger and marks my forehead, before she leans down and licks the place where she cut me.

MISTRESS ROGUE PATS our heads and leaves out the door, without even a goodbye.

Don't be Scared-Jordan

"YOU KNOW THAT ROGUE has to be close to the carnival, work here or something. There is no way she can just know where we are staying. Where we work? I am telling you that she is somewhere close, we just have to keep our eyes open for her." I start painting my face for the haunt. I love being a horror clown, it pays decent and free housing. We travel all through the year and it is how I met Mehki.

"I agree. I haven't noticed anyone that she could be though." He is putting on his neon green and black clown costume.

"We will figure it out, but for now it is time to go fuck up some kids and make them piss themselves." He laces up his boots and stands up as I put the last of my clown makeup on.

THEY REALLY NEED TO put some kind of air conditioner in here. It is so hot this summer, I can feel my makeup melting off. Hopefully, looking more ghastly than when I put it on. I hear the jumpscare from Mehki and get my fake ax ready for when the group passes in front of me. A young couple walks through and the woman is curled into the guy and hiding her eyes as he laughs and makes fun of her for being scared. Time to pay back the asshole for her. I swing out my ax in front of the guy. The girl yells and runs away as I back the guy into the wall. The guy has stopped laughing as I swing my ax back and purposely miss his head. I hear drips of wetness hitting the ground and look down. The guy has pissed himself and now I begin to laugh. I move my face closer to his and he turns his head away.

"I thought you guys weren't supposed to touch the customers." The pisser whimpers, as I place my hands on both sides of his head.

"Oh if I catch you laughing at your girl or mistreating her again. I will do more than that." I slap the metal behind his head then move back laughing as he takes off down the hallway.

I move back to the place that I hid and wait for the next patrons that have come to the funhouse for a scare. I fucking love this job! An hour later, I get my break and go out back and hope for the night to have cooled off a little bit. When I get outside I see Draven has Poppet bent over the side of the building and contemplate whether or not I should watch, however, I like my guts inside of my body so I turn around and walk back inside, where a blonde-haired girl is sitting in a chair drinking a soda. For some reason she seems familiar, but I am pretty sure I have never seen her before. She looks up from her phone and looks at me, a smile on her face and nods my direction. I wave to her as I head back into the funhouse and get ready for the next round of scares.

You, Him, and me Make three. -Rogue

I BELIEVE THIS OLD carousel music is driving me crazy, it's the same music day in and day out. Why the hell didn't I choose to do another ride? The day is busy, full of kids and adults alike, by the time the carnival closes, I am almost ready to pull out my hair. I close down the ride, and head back to my camper. I need some weed to help me wind down from the day. I go to the box where my stash is kept and pull out the plastic baggie and remove a few buds. I use my grinder and pour the contents of the grinded marijuana on my rolling board. I take a cone rolling paper out and use a small funnel to pour the grounded bud in, using a pink plastic rod to tap it all down. *Ah! Mary Jane, my best friend.* Once I get my cone filled up I twist the end and take a lighter to the end, inhaling the bitter smoke deep into my lungs and holding it there.

I begin coughing and release my breath. I turn on the television and begin to watch a television show as I finish toking on my joint. *Wonder what the guys are doing tonight?* I click the television off, not interested in anything that is on and decide to take a shower.

The steaming hot water feels so nice as it cascades down my body. I needed this. The calmness of the pot dulls my senses and I am relaxed. After I shower, I decide to put on a black,short dress and my bright ruby red lipstick. Time to go see my guys. I grab my black masquerade mask with the black feathers and high heels. My knife, baseball bat and a few toys go into a black bag. We are going to have so much fun tonight.

BEFORE I HAVE A CHANCE to knock, Mehki is at the door, he leans in the door frame with a fucking smirk on his sexy face. "Well, what do we have here?"

"Your worst fucking nightmare if you don't move your ass out of my way, Pet." I climb up on his steps, and he moves back, laughing.

"Well, come on in Mistress Rogue," Mehki says, as he walks across the room.

Jordan sits on the couch eating a sandwich, he looks up at me and grins. "Hi, Pup. Have you missed me?" I say, strolling up to him and patting him on his head.

"I did miss you. Are you here to play?" He places his food down on his plate and stands up, taking it to the kitchen.

"I have brought lots of toys to play with tonight, my boys." I drop the bag of toys on the ground and they both look at it.

"Who is ready for some fun?" I smile at the yearning I see in their eyes. *They are both ready for whatever I want to do to them.*

"Go get ready boys' I will set everything up in the bedroom," I say, picking up the bag and carrying it into the bedroom.

The guys' do as I say and begin undressing. They walk through the house, and into the shower and I get to work.

"WHAT THE FUCK ARE YOU going to do to us?" Mehki says, stepping out of the bathroom wearing nothing, but a towel.

"I think tonight we are going to have the best night ever!" I exclaim as I hold up a vibrating butt plug and some handcuffs.

Jordan steps out of the bathroom, his hair over his face, and looks up. There is plastic on the bed, and I am holding up the buttplug and handcuffs. "Mistress Rogue, are you going to handcuff me?"

"If you are a good boy, I will," I answer, taking some other items out of my bag.

"Lay down on the bed, Pup. On your back." I hand the cuffs to Mehki and he takes Jordan's wrist and puts the cuff on it.

"Put the other one the drawer loop. Theres no head board to cuff you too, Pup, so we have to make due." Mehki follows my instruction cuffing his boyfriend's wrist to bedside drawer.

I pull out a strap on from my bag, I snap it on and look up finding two eyes on me. "Haven't you seen a woman wear a strap before?"

" Yes." They both say in unison.

"Okay, well stop staring at me like that." I pull out a candle from my bag and a lighter, and light the wick.

"Hold this Pet, we will need that in a minute." I pull out my knife and place it on the bed.

"You two remember the safety word right?" The guy's both nod their head yes.

"Good. Now Pet, I want you to kiss Jordan, get him all turned on for me okay."

Mehki leans over and kisses Jordan passionately on his lips. I take the candle from him and begin dripping the liquid on Jordan's chest, before bringing it down his body. I drop a few drops on his dick that is hardening, before I wrap my hand around it. I use my hand to massage the candle drips that turn into oil on his cock, while smoothing the rest on his stomach. Jordan begins to take Mehki into his hand and I remove my hand from Jordan. I grab the bottle of Fuck Water lube and pour it in my hand, I massage the oil onto the strap dildo and pour some on Jordan's puckered hole. I push into him, going past the muscle, filling him up to the strap-on's hilt. I begin to thrust in and out, a moan escapes his lips as I am pleasuring him and he is pleasuring Mehki. "Don't let him cum."

"Come here Pet, Come fill me me up, I want you to fuck me while I am fucking Pup." Jordan lets go of Mehki and looks over at me. "Turn around."

Mehki turns around. "Bend over." I put lube on the vibrating butt plug and then push it into Mehki. A groan comes from him and he turns around.

"Are you liking this, Pup?" He nods his head with a smile on his face, from ear to ear. "You're such a good boy, taking everything I give."

Mehki steps behind me and lifts up my skirt, he sticks his hand between my thighs and runs his fingers through my folds and the wetness that is gathering there. "You're soaked."

"Shut up and fuck me, Pet." He pushes me down so I am over further on Jordan and places his hands on my hips.

I spread my legs giving him full access to enter me. When he pushes himself inside of me in one quick swoop I let out a moan. At first, the rythm was off, but soon we fuck each other in rythm Mehki fucking me as I fuck Jordan. Jordan wraps his hand around his cock as I push in and out of him, Mehki's hands wander all over my body and just when he feels me tightening up on him he reaches around and begins to stroke my clit. Before I know it Jordan starts coming, then me, and soon Mehki is reaching his climax.

Mehki pulls his cock out of me, and I pull out of Jordan. Mehki crashes on the bed beside Jordan and I remove the strap on, I will not need it the rest of the night. I climb up on the bed between the guys and kiss each one on their lips. Mehki takes his hand and runs it up my thigh and then in between my legs, gathering the results of his climaxing on his hand. He holds his come dripping fingers up to Jordan's mouth and he wraps his lips around Mehki's fingers and sucks them clean. Tasting both Mehki and I, Mehki places his hand back between my legs and begins fingering me as I run my hands along both guys' cocks. Wanting to make them hard again. Mehki's fingers feel so good filling me, and when I start to moan, he leans over swallowing my pleasure with his kiss. When his lips leaves mine, I turn to face Jordan and kiss him deeply, my tongue exploring his mouth. I use the key and free his hand out of the cuff and he takes his free hand and begins to move his where Mehki is finger fucking me. Jordan places his fingers on my clit and begins massaging me and in no time I am coming again.

Both guys are hard now, "I want you both at the same time."

I wrap my leg over Jordan's, Mehki removes his hand and grabs Jordan's cock and brings his tip to my pussy. He guides his boyfriend into me and when Jordan bucks his hips I can feel him all the way in. I feel something cold hit my backside and realize it's the lube, Mehki uses his fingers to massage my asshole, and begins to insert his fingers in me, readying me for his cock.

"Fuck me, Pet. I am ready," I tell him and he removes his fingers and glides his dick in between my folds before he enters me.

The feeling is overwhelming. I am full and they work me hard, both thrusting in me as we kiss and and move and enjoy each other's touch, kiss, and bodies. In unison they thrust into me, the feeling is sensational, I have never felt so used, but yet in control my whole damn life. When Jordan begin's rubbing my clit I know that I will not last long, He thrust into my pussy, as Mehki takes my ass with no abandon, the three of us fufliflling a need deep within us and soon I come so hard I see fucking stars. Jordan follows after me and then Mehki, each chasing their pleasure, their release, both filling me up with their come. Mehki reaches over and kisses my shoulder, before he removes his cock out of my ass. Jordan stays in me a bit longer, just holding me close and kissing my forehead.

I kiss his lips and move away from him before making my way out of the bed. This time I take the knife out of my bag and slice open my own hand and gather the blood with my finger and mark them both with the letter A on their foreheads.. They are mine now. They belong to me, I've claimed them, marked them with my own life force and neither one of them will ever get away. I kiss them both before I gather my items. And walk out the door, without saying goodbye.

Ours- Mehki

"WE NEED TO FIND OUT who our girl is, Jordan. This is bullshit. She comes here almost every night, uses us, treats us like her play toys then disappears. I'm fucking tired of this." I use my thumb and gather blood from Jordan's forehead, I place my thumb in my mouth, my hand still has the taste of her pussy on it and now no matter what she is in me, her blood is a part of me, it's almost as if we are one.

I use the same thumb and wipe my forehead, and bring it to Jordan's mouth so he can taste what I'm tasting so he can have her in him too, so we all three can be as if we are all one. "I believe tht she knows we belong to her, she marked us. She's claimed us Mehki, now we need to do what we can to figure this out. We must seem like fucking idiots. I did see a girl that reminded me of her in the break room the other day. I know I've seen her around, I'm pretty sure she runs the carousel or one of the other kiddie rides. I think that tomorrow, before we work in the funhouse. We go scope out the kiddie rides, see if you think it is our Mistress Rogue or not."

"Let's do it." I pull him to the bed and we climb into the come covered bed and I wrap my arms around Jordan. "Tomorrow we are getting our girl."

IT WAS LATE WHEN WE woke up, almost three o'clock. We scramble to shower, and get dressed before we head to observe the rides around the carnival. We know our little masked vixen is around here somewhere, the problem is where. How will we know where to find her? How will we know it's her? Surely, her appearance isn't much different than her Mistress Rogue persona, we know her vocal tones from commanding all the way to her screaming our names with pleasure. We know the shape of her lips, the way they smile, the way they command, the way they taste, intimately. Her body, we know every curve, everything about her besides what she looks like under those goddamn masks. Finding her should be as easy as making Jordan suck my cock, which is pretty fucking easy.

The carnival grounds are scarce, just a few carnies getting their games and rides ready for the evening. A few acquaintances say hi as Jordan and me pass by. The sun is beating down hard today, summers here in Kentucky seem to get ridiculously hot. I wipe the sweat from my brow, as I make my way to the airplane ride. I don't spot any workers near-by, the last person I've known to be incharge of this ride is Marcus, a twenty-something year old that we hired for the summer. A clanging has me glaring around, trying to see who caused the noise. A dark-tanned man with black hair is tightening up a loose bolt on the back side of the ride. I hold my hand up and wave to the guy, before stomping away.

"I'm telling you, Mehki. I've seen a girl with glasses that look just like her. I know she is around here somewhere. I think we should check the slides next, then maybe the carousel." Jordan begins to trudge toward the gigantic slides, where children, and adults sometimes, use old potato sacks to ride down the curvy metal ride.

To the right about a hundred yards is a short woman, who is talking to another person. Her mannerisms are familiar, the way she talks while moving her arms, excitedly as if her arms are in a race that her body knows nothing about. A pair of black glasses adorn her face and her long, straight dishwater blonde hair is in a messy knot upon her head.

"Jordan! Come here." I motion for him to come back to where I'm standing. "Look at the girl standing there. Doesn't she look familiar to you?"

Jordan peers at where I'm pointing and a huge grin comes over his face. "Told you I fucking seen her around the carousel before. That is the same girl that was in the break room I was telling you about. That is Mistress Rogue, I'm fucking telling you." We watch as the girl sways off from the guy, done with the conversation. The guy stares at her ass as she walks away and it takes everything in me from not going over there and kicking his ass.

"That motherfucker!" Jordan screams, starting to trudge through the carnival. I run after him.

"Don't worry about him, we will take care of him later. I've got a plan. It's time for Mistress Rogue, to bow down to us for a change." A wicked smile shows across Jordan's face as I fill him in on my plans.

Where did she go?- Jordan

THE NIGHT SEEMS TO take forever to end. Once the last few ppl exit the funhouse, Mehki and I run to the closet where we stash our masks. Mehki is wearing a purge venom mouth that lights up in blue, a sickening grin is painted on it with blue LED lights that light up once you push the button, there are X's for eyes that light up blue as well.

I slip on my leather plague doctor bird mask and zip up my hoodie cloaking myself in all black. I'm not one hundred percent on board with the plan that Jordan has orchestrated, but I'm going along with it anyway. We rush towards the carousel, where she should now just be closing up. I move behind the circle of horses, but she is nowhere to be found. We start toward the campers that house the summer employees when a scream from the adjourning forest screeches through the night air. I stop immediately and look toward where Mehki is, with no words needing to be said, he dashes through the games with me following behind him.

The forest is dense and dark and you can't see very far in front of you. The sound of someone trudging through the foliage can be heard, a rusting noise as if someone is fighting and the noise of broken branches can be heard. We are running as fast as we can, deeper into the thickness, when a dark menacing voice can be heard. "Stop fighting me you cunt. Don't think for a minute I won't cut off your god damn head and fuck you in the hole thats left."

I'm not a fucking bear, so why are you taking me to the woods?-Ann

THE DAY'S HEAT IS GONE and the night's cooler breeze hits my face as I lock up the gate to the carousel. Today has been long and rough, with one kid up chucking on another. I hate when that happens, then I have to spray off the ride and stop it for enough time, while hateful assholes stand in line bitching. I would let them walk in the vomit of the person, but it's against the rules, someone might slip and fall and sue.

I just want to go home, take a nice cold shower, smoke a little weed, and then perhaps go to my guys' camper for a little sexual relaxation.

The lights that are usually bright at night are out as I trek through the carnival, all the rides and games are locked up for the night. Cleaning up the mess has made me late getting back to my camper. I turn to go behind the games toward where the summer worker's campers are located when a hand reaches out and grabs me. An arm pulls me back into them the smell of alcohol mixed with chewing tobacco invades my nostrils and makes me want to vomit. I would know that stench from anywhere, fucking Judd. Judd is the guy who runs the water gun clown game. The one where you squirt water into the clown's mouth to fill a balloon.

He begins dragging me towards the woods, I fight and kick at it to no avail. Who would have ever thought the fat bastard would be so damn strong?

"STOP FIGHTING ME YOU cunt. Don't think for a minute I won't cut off your god damn head and fuck you in the hole thats left." He practically grunts menacingly into my ear.

THERE IS NO WAY THAT this disgusting excuse for a human being is going to do anything to me. I will let him take me wherever he is going and once we are there I will knee him in his balls and run back to the carnival. Damn it! I wish I had my trusty baseball bat, I would make this guy pay big time for even thinking he could put his sausage link fingers on me. Judd is grunting, running out of steam as he drags me. I can hear his overexertion, his lack of breathing and wheezing. He is libel to fall over dead from the exercise of this much walking.

We stop suddenly and I look around and see a blue light in the distance, but I can't make out what it is. Maybe someone seen this jerk off take me into the woods and they called the cops? I hope so. He still holds me close to him and with the hand that isnt wrapped around my mouth he rips my shirt my breast is still covered by my bra but I am still exposed. *I try to use my teeth to bite down on his hand as I try to scream for help, my yelling is muffled by his huge hand. He is gonna pay big time for every time he has touched me, believe that.*

He slides his disgusting fingers under my bra, and begins to play with my nipples, tugging on them. I use my foot and stamp down as hard as I can on his foot. He is wearing boots though, so all he does is laugh and pinches my nipple harder.

"Oooh yeah I like it when you wiggle baby, you are just making me harder." He breathes into my ear.

I choke on vomit. Fuck! What can I do? This guy is about two hundred fifty pounds heavier than me. What can I do to get away? Think Ann. Think. I think of everything I have learned in self defense. Stomp the feet, elbow in the gut, pull the dick like a lawn mower that needs started, then run. I stomp his foot again. He does absolutely nothing. I swing my arm as much as I can with the way he is holding me and unfortunately he just holds me tighter. I try gliding my hand to his crotch, but I can't reach his cock to pull it. I'm so screwed, and not in a good way.

My eyes dart around, looking for anything I can use as a weapon. Anyway, I can get free. I'm starting to panic now, I'm seriously being kidnapped and about to be raped by an alcoholic middle age man that couldn't smell as bad as if he wallowed in a dumpster.

What would Rogue do? Rogue would have her bat with her, dumbass. Think, think, Think!

A cracking of branches can be heard from behind us. Someone or something is in these woods with us. I hope it's a bear, It can attack him and I will run like there is a zombie apocalypse and I'm about to be ate alive.

A groan hits my ear and I feel warm wetness run down my back. Judds' grip loosens on me and I don't even look back at what had happened. I take flight toward the opening in the woods where we ascended. And run straight into a masked man. He grabs me and holds me to him. I would know his Versace Eros cologne from anywhere. Mehki. I melt into his arms as they envelope me.

"Rogue, did he hurt you?" Mehki's voice vibrates in my ear as I start to calm down. I use his shirt to dry the tears I didn't even realize that I was crying.

I want to tell him no, but the words won't come out. I shake my head no. He looks over my shoulder at what I'm assuming is Judd's body and Jordan.

I feel Jordan wrap his arms around us, holding us both. We are all covered in the blood of my kidnapper. I peer up at my saviors, and when Jordan removes his mask and slams his lips on mine, I take what he gives me, his tongue discovering my mouth as Mehki's hands begin to roam my body. My nipples begin to pebble against my bra as I feel Mehki undoing the clasp. Mehki's hand slides down playing with the waist of my shorts as Jordan is nibbling at my neck making his way down kissing, nibbling, and licking before taking my puckered bud into his mouth. A slight moan escapes my mouth as I relax into my men. Mehki unbuttons my shorts, letting them glide to the ground before he rips my panties off of me and flips me around tearing Jordan's lips from me. Mehki's mouth crashes on me, taking my lips hard, his teeth biting down causing blood to pour from my mouth, he pulls away and gathers the blood on his finger and lifts it to my forehead where he draws and M and a J.

"You belong to us now, our little Hellion," he growls before lifting me up. The sound of Jordan removing his pants and Mehki working himself out can be heard throughout the woods.

Blood stained baby batter- Jordan

Our little Rogue is being so brave, but I know that she is scared. She has to be. I move silently throughout the opening, sneaking up behind him, I hear the sound of Rogue's shirt being ripped the sound echoing through the woods. *That piece of shit will pay for that. He will pay for even thinking he can touch what belongs to Mehki and me.*

The knife I always carry on me glints in the moonlight casting a light. I lift the knife as I fist the hair thats left on Judd's balding head and rake my knife along his neck. Blood gushes out flowing onto Rogue's back as soon as the pig lets her go she takes off to the opening in the woods. Judd's body hits the ground, with a thump, the life leaving his eyes. I bed down over top of him and with both hands cradling the knife I shove the blade into his heart.

I gaze up to see where my loves are standing. Mehki is cradling our Rogue in his arms as I trudge toward them. I need them in my arms, to feel them, to touch them. I need Rogue to know she is ours, she belongs to us, at that we will do anything...*fucking anything* to keep her. I peek down at the blood that is covering me, soaking through my shirt and rip my shirt off. I leave the tattered mess on the ground as I slide behind our girl, she turns to face me and I take her lips with mine. Her tongue tastes like mint gum that is fading away, I devour her kissing, sucking, licking, and biting down her lips, her chin, her neck, all down her chest until I take her nipple into my mouth. A few moments after taking her between my lips, she is ripped from me, turned to face Mehki.

You're such a good girl for us- Mehki

I glide my hand down cupping her pussy with my palm, working my fingers into her, pumping in and out of her as Jordan's hands slide to Rogue's breast as he pulls and pinches her pink buds. Her juices flow through my fingers as I work them up and begin massaging her clit. Her body is so reactive to our touch as she begins to come undone, Jordan moves closer to us, taking me into his hand as I lift our little Rogue, he positions both our cocks close together before lining us up to her delicious wet pussy, I lower her down slowly, as she takes us both gasping and groaning with every inch. She throws her head back, her mouth in an O as I kiss her chest that is bare before me.

"You're such a good girl, Rogue. Taking us both in your hot, wet cunt." A moan slips from her lips as I take them once again swallowing her pleasure.

"Such a good girl," Jordan agrees, I can feel his cock gliding with mine as we work ourselves in and out of her, both thrusting simultaneously.

Grunts, groans, and moans fill the air, radiating from all three of us. A feeling of completion, of being whole running over me. I have never felt like this before. Not with Jordan, not with anyone else, because Rogue is the one who completes us. She is ours.

I place my hand betweens us, pinching her clit and she immediately cums, soaking both of our cocks. Jordan follows right after, filling her full of him, and soon I join in my release escaping me, all of us spent.

Jordan glides out of her first, then me, still holding her close to me. Jordan kisses me on my lips, over Rogue's shoulder and of course I kiss him back. He slides his hand between her thighs and pulls out our cum, it glistens from the moonlight on his fingers before he holds it to her mouth, she opens them, taking his fingers and cleans them off, once he pulls them from her lips with a pop, he pulls out a knife from his pocket, the one he used on Judd and brings it up to Rogue's chest. He gives her time to stop him, before raking the blade across her chest marking her with a J before handing me the knife. I take it, her eyes peering up at me before I too, mark her with an M. Jordan gathers her in his embrace before I rip open my shirt and cut an A into my flesh. My gaze turns to Jordan, with a silent nod, he gives me permission to mark him too. An A is carved into Jordan's chest before I close the knife and hand it back to him.

"You belong to us now, Mistress Rogue." A smirk shows on her face as she gathers us both in her arms.

"And you belong to me."

A moment passes before Jordan looks around and opens his mouth. "What the fuck are we going to do with that bastards body?"

I take a deep breath and let it out. I know what exactly needs to be done, but I hate the fact that we have to do it. It's time to seek out the expertise of Draven, if anyone knows how to get rid of a body without it being found. It's definitely him.

Chagrin is a bitch- Ann

"SO YOU, GUY'S DON'T even want to know what the A stands for? It could mean asshole, awful, or a small dick. You just carved the letter in yourselves not even knowing," I say, tromping through the forest toward the carnival.

Mehki let me use his shirt to cover myself since my clothes were either ripped or covered in a dead man's blood.

"It meant something to you, Hellion. That is all that matters. You would draw an A on us. You marked us with it. That's all that matters." Jordan walks beside me, my hand in his as Mehki walks in front of us, guiding us back to the safety of the carnival.

Mehki stops mid-stride and turns on his heel to face us. "Since you mention it. What does the A mean?"

I clear my throat before peering up at him. "It stands for Ann. My real name is Ann." A smile forms on his face before he kisses me on my forehead.

"Our sexy Ann," he says before turning back around and continuing walking. Jordan brings my hand up to his lips still holding it and kisses the back.

Once we make it through the woods about twenty minutes later, we head to the back of the carnival where Draven and Poppet's camper is located. We go through the ten or fifteen that is out front and make it to the back. Mehki bangs on the aluminum door and stands back.

"What the fuck do you bitches want?" Draven bites out as he answers the door. He slams back hitting the side of the camper with a thump. He is wearing nothing but a pair of sleeping pants, his abnormally white skin shining in the moonlight, his tattoo's seeming to glow. His sleep pants riding his waist showing off a very nice V at his hips. Poppet comes to the door all smiles.

"Don't be rude, Draven. They have come to play." Poppet Draven's overly happy wife says almost pushing him out of the way as she peeks out the door. "Look at you! You're covered in blood! I like blood." She giggles as her eyes rake over me.

"We need your help, Drave. You know this is the last place I want to come ask for help, but you're the only person we know would even fucking know what to do." Mehki looks embarrassed having to ask Draven for help. It makes me curious as to what kind of story these two have. I peek over at Jordan who is still holding my hand, tightly, his head peering down at the ground.

"What makes you think I would help you two?" Draven crosses his arms over his chest giving Mehki a death glare that makes me want to slink back a little.

I have never talked to Draven, but Poppet waves at me from time to time, always a smile on her face. Always seemingly happy.

"Judd attacked Ann, dragged her into the woods, tried to rape her. We killed him. We need help getting rid of the body." Jordan peers up and looks Draven in the eyes. "We don't know what to do with it."

"WELL, WHY DIDN'T YOU say so!" Draven says, turning around and kissing Poppet. "My little Poppet, why don't you and Ann get her cleaned up, while we go take care of that fat bastard."

Poppet peers up at him with a sad look on her face. "But I want to go see what he looks like."

"Don't be sad my little Poppet. I will tell you every detail when I return." He takes her chin in his hand and tips her face up to his, forcing her eyes to meet his. "I will be back soon, don't be sad. Look you have a new friend." Draven points to me before he goes back into the house and in a few minutes, he returns wearing a black jacket, jeans, boots, and a cigarette hanging from his lips.

Jordan holds me to him first, before kissing me and then Mehki grabs me from him, his tongue pushing it's way through my lips taking what is his. I will let him think he is in charge for now, but when this mess is cleaned up, I'm going to have to remind him who is in charge.

"We will be back soon, Hellion," he says, kissing my forehead one last time and walking away.

"Hi, I'm Poppet, but you can call me Serenity." The beautiful dark haired woman holds out her hand to me and I take it. "Come on, let's get you a shower and some clean clothes."

She nods, and I climb up the three stairs into her camper. "Thank you."

A whistle comes from behind me."Hello beautiful." I turn around and a white bird is there moving his head up and down flapping his wings.

"Wylie, are you flirting with our guest?" Poppet says walking up to the bird. She pats the flirty bird on the head and kisses it. " Behave you naughty boy."

"Naughty boy," The adorable bird repeats. I can't help but to smile at the antics.

My eyes flutter around looking at the small camper. It is relatively clean with pictures of what I'm assuming are favorite horror movies on the wall. Skulls and dark clown items seem to be the decoration for their living space. Black, purples, and neon green painted as if you stepped into a dark carnival. I absolutely love the gothic, emo themed home.

"The shower is right through there. I will get you some clothes and toiletries so you can clean up." Poppet starts digging through a small cabinet and picks out some clothes and lays it on the sink in the small bathroom. A towel and wash cloth is laying on top. "There is shampoo and conditioner and some vanilla bath wash in there. Do you need any help? I can wash you off, if you need me too." I shake my head and step up into the space toward where she nodded her head.

"I think I can manage. Thank you," I say, looking down at the blood stained clothes I'm wearing.

The bathroom closely resembles mine, it's small with a half size tub. There is a shower though, so that is good. The water turns pink as it cascades down my body and out the drain. I'm so glad that Poppet let me wash the blood off. I could have went back to my camper, but I needed to scrub it off as quickly as possible, even though I don't think there is enough water in the world to scrub the feeling of his paws on me. Once I scrub myself once or twice but three times, I turn off the water and use the towel that Poppet laid out for me.

The clothes were too long for me, Poppet is clearly close to six feet tall, making my five foot five stature feel like I'm fun sized. I saunter out of the bathroom and through to the hallway.

"Can I throw these away?" I am holding my bloody clothes wrapped up into a ball in front of me.

"Honey, I think we should probably burn those. I am pretty sure that is evidence. Here is some sandals you can wear." She grabs a lighter from a drawer in the kitchen before trudging my way.

"Put these on and follow me." she grabs the clothes out of my grasp and makes her way to the camper's entrance. I do as I'm told and follow the tall, dark-haired woman out the door.

A MAGNIFICENT BLAZE grows before my eyes as I watch my clothes go up in flames. "You know I've seen you someplace before. I'm from here. I think you were a couple years ahead of me in school maybe." She squeezes a white bottle of lighter fluid over the top of the fire the flames to roll higher.

"Ann Wilson, that's my name." My eyes drawl over her as she stands staring at the fire as if she is in a trance.

"No, I know you from the funhouse. I've seen you there making those guys fall on their knees and worship you. Talent, pure fucking talent. They beg you to put them in their place, their divine devotion to you in that space, in that moment it's unreal." A smile comes to her face as she pulls out a knife, from where? I have no idea considering she is wearing a small cami and shorts and begins to take the point of the blade and dig it in the tip of her finger. "But, if you think for one second you can bat those pretty long lashes Draven's way, you will lose your eyeballs because I will cut them out and shove them down your throat before I cut your heart out and feed it to Wylie. Do we have an understanding?" My mouth falls open and I stare in shock at the psychopath my guy's have left me with.

"Uh huh," I say, before clearing my throat.

"Great! I know we are going to be the best of friends!" The knife disappears once again before she claps her hand back into a giddy mood, she rushes to me and hugs me.

"Bestest friends," I repeat as I let her arms engulf me and hold me close to her chest.

Being an Asshole Cost him an Arm & a Leg- Mehki

THE NIGHT IS DARK, the moon is shining an evil glow surrounds us. Draven being the psychopath he is and knowing exactly what we needed dug out a small hatchet, some black tarp and a few shovels from a storage building we use on the property. Jordan said absolutely nothing as we began trudging back through the woods toward where the bastard's body lay.

After about twenty minutes of walking we finally make it back to the body. Draven runs over to the body and swiftly kicks Judd in the side.

"Fucking prick!" Draven calls, before his eyes turn toward us. "Don't just stand there, help me chop him up."

Jordan's face tints to an almost slimy green before he reluctantly plods to stand beside Draven. "We need to make sure he cannot ever be found. So Take your knife out and fuck up his hands. Make sure that his fingerprints can never be recognized." Jordan pulls the same blade out of his pocket he used on Judd then later on Rogue and begins slicing through the cadaver's flesh.

"I think we should hide his body in different holes even taking some of him away from this forest. Maybe his head and torso and dump them off a bridge in different locations." I chime in, walking toward them. Blood splashes as they begin to slice and dice Judd. I go off deeper into the woods carrying a shovel with me. Once I find a good spot, I begin to dig a hole deep enough to where a piece of his body will never be found.

I DIG A HOLE ABOUT three feet deep and two feet deep before quitting. Sweat drips from my forehead and runs down my face and I use my shirt to wipe it off. Damn hot summer nights, I look at the moon above, a cloud covering it making it hard to see, before I trek back to where Jordan and Draven are almost finished dismembering Judd. That old man was always a pervert, but I never expected he would try that shit. Well, guess he will be spending his days in hell getting butt fucked by a giant stuffed teddy bear like he sales at his stupid game.

"I have a hole ready for a bit of him," I say picking up a black trash bag full of visera and not telling what else. "I will go bury this shit. Be back."

Jordan's sapphire eyes look dark and sad, I can tell he is grossed the fuck out, I mean anyone with half sanity would be, but he doesn't say a word, just nods his head. *It makes me wonder if he thinks what he done was worth saving Ann over. Or if him taking care of Judd was a bad thing. If you ask me, I say the motherfucker got what he deserves and there is no telling how many women he has hurt that noone knew anything about it.*

When I get back to the hole I throw the bag in and begin shoveling, filling it up with lose dirt. Once it is full, I pat the top with the shovel to flatten out the soil and then get a shovel full of debri and cover the hole. That's one part of that dirty ol' fucker that will never be found.

Blood, Guts, and Gore, Oh My!- Jordan

THE STENCH OF SWEAT, vicera, and the metallic smell of blood infiltrate my nostrils. I choke back the vomit that is dying to spew, I can't be weak about this. *I killed a man, I took his life to save our Rogue. It had to be done.* Now, I must face the consequences of my actions and help dispose of the body.

The ripping, tearing, and squishing noises that come with dismembering the bodies does nothing to help the uneasiness of the whole situation. Who would have ever thought that not even an hour after a person dies thier body would start decomposing and already giving off a stench that would bring tears to your eyes?

"Bag that arm," Draven growls, as he raises the hatchet above his head and swipes down a blow that immediately cuts Judd's leg off at the knee. "We need to get this shit done, I need to get back to my Poppet."

Blood is covering his handsome face, I never looked at Draven sexually before and even though this might sound serial killer crazy, the splashes of blood covering his face in torso just adds to his sexiness. That is a thought I would definitely keep to myself. Not that he would mind being admired by a man, but if Poppet found out, I would end up in worse shape than Judd. She is definitely protective over her man.

I do what Draven commands and place the rather heavy arm into the bag, we cut off his fingers and hand placing his body parts in different bags, so that the parts of him would be mixed and matched if ever found. Which we clearly pray to whatever divinity that might exist would never be found.

I hear footsteps approaching and look up after tying off the leg-filled trash bag and see Mehki stomping toward us. "Got one buried. I will take another to the left and bury it then we can take a few around town and the next city over and drop them off bridges."

"You two can manage to do that without fucking up I'm sure." Draven eyes us both and looks down at what is left of the body. "You can use Poppet's car, but you fucknuts better not leave a trace of blood in it or you will be the next person I chop up."

"Draven, this goes without saying, but thank you for helping us. I know shit hasn't been cool between us in a long time, it's our fault. We owe you one." Mehki's voice is thick as he picks up the bag containing Judd's leg and throws it over his shoulder.

"Yes, you do." Draven draws back the ax and with a thump starts hacking into Judd's torso.

Mehki heads back toward the left of us in the woods, and I use my knife to cut up the feet of Judd, I don't know if they can identify a person by footprints, but I will not take a chance with it.

Thirty minutes later, we are trekking through the woods back to the carnival site. All of us are carrying bags full of Judd. Time to drop him in different locations and get this foolishness behind us.

My heroes-Ann

POPPET HAS SAT DORMANT for the last fifteen minutes just
staring at the flames. She was mesmerized by the fire, my clothes being
engulfed and swallowed by the black ashes. I, on the other hand, feel like
I'm coming apart at the seams. I'm a nervous wreck and by the time I see
my guys and Draven placing black trash bags into a car, I feel as though
I'm going to crumble. This has been a long, dirty, disgusting day and I
really just need Pet and Pup to hold me.

Mehki saunters up to me first, a dark look is written all over his
gorgeous face, his eyes are expressionless and I can't even manage to
think about what all they had to do out in the forest. Jordan comes up
to me next his whole body covered in blood. He collapses in front of me
and places his head in my lap. I run my fingers through his long, blonde
hair hoping to ease whatever darkness has infiltrated him out there.

"Thank you for saving me Pup," I coo, hoping he will look me in the
eyes, because I'm wanting to know that he isn't disgusted with me. He
nods his head, but never faces me.

"We have to go dispose of some trash," Draven says to Poppet,
grabbing her up from the chair she is resting in and she gladfully jumps
into his arms and wraps her legs around him.

"Not without me! You have been away for long enough." She doesn't
give him time to object before she has her mouth on his, and he moves
her toward the camper her back slamming against it as she gyrates on
him. The blood covering him not stopping her from attacking him.

I have seen sex in every position, every way imaginable, but seeing
those two go at it, dry humping each other gets my panties wet. Maybe
I'm a psychopath too. Mehki bends down and takes my lips with his, his
tongue invading my mouth, taking what he needs from me and I'm free
to give it.

Jordan finally stares up at me a look of lust and longing in his eyes.
"We need to go, ya'll can fuck later, we need to get this done now." That

is the first time since I've met him that he has took charge. He climbs up from the ground and pulls me out of the chair as Mehki moves out of his way he pulls me close to him and holds me, wrapping his arms tightly around me, almost sucking the air from my lungs.

"I will never let anyone hurt you, Ann," Jordan whispers in my ear as his fingers brush down my back.

Splash- Mehki

I PULL OUT A BAG OF Judd from the trunk of Poppet's new silver Kia rio and scramble to the middle of the bridge. I peer down at the water below, it's rolling pretty good so maybe whatever body parts happen to be in this bag will get swept down the river. I hang the bag over the side and let my grip go as the bag falls into water with a resounding splash. That fucking asshole is gonna be fish food and to be honest, winding up as fish shit is probably the best thing to ever happen to the old man.

I climb into the backseat and pull Ann into my lap and hold her close to me. She rests her head on my shoulder as her hand wraps around Jordan's. I can tell that what happened in the woods has taken its toll out on him and I know after we get rid of the other two bags and go home. I'm going to have to console him, quiet his demons and let him know that everything will be alright. If anyone ever does find out about what happened, he would not be in trouble for any of it. I would take full responsibility of it all. There would be no way that he or Ann would ever see punishment for the justice that was served tonight. My eyes go from Jordan to Ann and cannot help but to notice how full my heart fills. Like this is what I have been missing for so long. I kiss our girl chastly on the lips and then my guys. How I feel might be untraditional but it's the realist, genuine feeling I have ever felt in my entire life.

Mine-Jordan

WE DROPPED OFF THE last of Judd into two different counties so hopefully he won't be found. Draven and Poppet has been cozying up the front seat and making out the entire time. I'm pretty sure their night will be full of adrenaline fueled passion. I look over at Mehki and Ann, her eyes are closed as she rests her head on Mehki's shoulder, her hand still wrapped in mine and I peer up at Mehki. He looks tired, the events of the day taking the fight out of him.

Draven pulls up to our camper to let us out and I move to take Ann from Mehki's lap pulling her into my arms as he climbs out of the backseat.

"THAT WAS FUN, WE NEED to do that again sometime," Draven shouts out the window as Mehki unlocks the metal door leading into the camper.

"I hope the fuck not." was my only reply. Draven takes off leaving nothing but dirt and debris flying.

Ann begins to stir once I hand her up to Mehki and wraps her arms around his neck. "Come on, Hellion let's get you to bed while me and Jordan clean up."

Mehki places Ann in the middle of the bed and covers her up, she stirs in the bed, but quickly falls back asleep. I can't help but to watch them, admire them, somewhere between being Rogue's pup and dismembering her attacker she has become ours. We all belong to each other. My heart swells in my chest knowing that both of them are mine. Just like I belong to them.

Wakey, Wakey- Ann

THE SUN HASN'T RISEN, yet. I rise up in the bed, realizing where I am. I must have fallen asleep, last night was a hell of a night and drained every bit of energy from me. Pup and Pet are sleeping soundly one on each side of me, I have never felt so secure, so protected before. I turn over and face Jordan, his eyes are fluttering as if he is dreaming. I use my finger tip to trace his perfect cupid bow lips, before reaching forward and kissing them. My hand slowly glides down his body, past the waist of his boxers as I take his cock into my hand. His eyes open then a smile on his face as he sees it's me who is touching him.

"Good morning, Hellion," his voice is rough with sleep, husky and deep and sexy.

"It's about to be," I reply as I use my other hand to do the same thing to Mehki who is lying behind me asleep.

A few strokes of his dick and he is awake too, kissing the back of my head as I work them both simultaneously. Mehki pulls his cock out of my hand before making his way to the foot of the bed, dragging my panties and pants from me. I slip off my shirt, my best bra free.

"Sit up Ann and spread your legs wide." I glare at him. I'm going to have to remind him that I'm the boss here, not him. I still do as he says though. "Stand up Jordan. Our little Rogue is about to be fucked in the mouth while I eat that cunt of hers."

Jordan climbs up on the bed, his head almost reaching the ceiling as he uses the wall to balance himself in front of me. His cock is right where it needs to be as I peer up at him licking my lips ready to taste Jordan before they flicker to Mehki, waiting on instructions. "Make him feel good, Hellion. Show me how you like to suck dick."

My tiny hand wraps around Jordan's length as I pump his already hard cock. My thumb swipes a drop of precum as I work it over his mushroom head. I lean forward taking him into my mouth all the way to the hilt and back up. A groan leaves his mouth, clearly enjoying my mouth on him.

"Lean all the way back, Hellion. Brace your head on the wall. Jordan I want you to hold her head and fuck her face." I do as he says leaning all the way back while Jordan fixes himself infront of me. I open my mouth and he runs his cock along my bottom lip before entering my warm wanton mouth.

Mehki slides up between my legs, I'm sure he can smell my arousal before he even got close to my pussy, I am dying needing him, wanting to be touched. My cunt is wet and wanting. He flattens his tongue running up the slit before taking my clit in between his lips and sucking me hard. My hands hold on to Jordan, my nails digging into his ass, hard enough to mark them. He tastes sweet, like cotton candy mixed with salt. I know that without a doubt, I could enjoy eating him every morning for breakfast. Noises are coming from both of them as Jordan pounds into my mouth and Mehki is filling me up with his fingers. The sound of their pleasure has me thrusting my hips taking him in as far as I can while Jordan's cock drives to the back of my throat, making it hard to breathe. Tears escape my eyes as he face fucks me, using my mouth as his pleasure hole.

Stickler for a Fisting- Mehki

I MOVE MY HAND AND begin sticking my fingers into one by one, stretching her, opening her hot, wet, cunt adding fingers as I suck her throbbing clit. Her wetness is pouring from her as I begin using my whole hand to fill her up, making a fist inside of her. A moan comes from her, Jordan's cock keeping her from yelling as her juices flood from her covering my hand and the bed. I thrust my hand in her, so she can feel all of me, ramming inside her, I pull out and do it again and again. She takes my fist like a good girl. She squirts, her juices flowing again, as I pull my hand from her and begin licking up her cum.

Jordan's head goes back as he finishes inside her mouth and when he pulls out his jizz is running out of her mouth. Like the good girl she is, she licks her lips, cleaning him from her. He bends down and gathers his juice from her chest that had leaked out of her mouth and takes his finger to his lips tasting himself. A look of pleasure watches over them both. I climb up the bed and begin to lick the rest of Jordan's cum off her titties before kissing my way up her throat and once I make it to her mouth, I force my tongue in. Taking her lips, kissing and biting and licking them. When I start to pull away, I bite down on her bottom lip causing blood to flow. I run my finger down gathering her blood on it and bring it up to my forehead where I mark an A and a J.

I drag Anne down on the bed, turning her over in one fell swoop. Her face is into the bed as I grab her hips and bring her ass up. I use my tongue and work it around her asshole, licking and sucking at the delicate skin before placing my fingers in. She wiggles and pushes back into me as finger her ass hole stretching it, preparing it for us. Jordan watches his eyes full of lust as he slides into the bed beside me, taking me into one hand and massaging her clit with the other.

"Both of you have been so good, I think you deserve a treat," I praise removing my fingers from her ass and kneeling behind her. Jordan is already hard again and ready as our cocks meet at her openings. I enter her ass as he moves situating himself he has a bottle of lube in his hand he flips open and pours generously down her crack as I take her it runs down on my cock making it easier for me to pound into her. Jordan's dick moves with mine slowly as he enters her ass with me us fucking her tight puckered hole in rhythm. She groans and thrust her hips back into us.

"Faster. Harder," she begs and we do as we are told fucking her ass like it would be the last thing we ever do.

In only a few minutes Jordan pulls out of her and begins stocking his cock, harder and harder and I know when a growl leaves his mouth that he is about to erupt. Jordan's cum comes out thick and he squirts it all over her as ass crack running down onto my cock much like the lube and I fill her ass hole full of him.

He falls to the bed spent, only using his hand massaging and pulling on her clit as she soon comes, her ass hole tightens around me sending me into my own orgasm. I fall over her kissing her shoulders and then to the side I wrap my arms around her as Jordan joins us taking us both in his arms and this is how we all three fall asleep intertwined and spent.

Breaking News- Jordan

THE SUN IS SHINING directly in my eyes waking me up. The scent of
sex and cologne fills my nostrils as I sit up and yawn. Phones are going off
like crazy, ringing, messages and notifications one right after the other. I
crawl to the end of the bed and pick up my phone that is on a charger. I
flip through the notifications, when a call comes through jolting me.

"Hello?"

"Jordan, you and Mehki need to come to BJ's camper, there is some
shit that is going down and all the workers need to be here for it." Joe,
one of the game workers says sending me into instant panic mode.

"What's going on?" I ask, keeping my voice straight, hoping he will
fill me in before cops start pounding on our door.

"Y'all get your asses down here. That's all I know to tell ya." The
phone call ends abruptly, the sound of silence on the other line.

"You need to wake up, get your clothes on. Joe called and said that
we needed to go to BJ's camper that it's important!" I almost scream,
terrified that what happened last night is coming back to bite me on my
ass.

"What?" a sleepy sexy voice asks, as she sits up in bed wiping the hair
out of her face. Damn even with freshly fucked hair and sleep in her eyes
she is the sexiest woman I have ever laid eyes on.

"We need to go!" She peers at me her eyes going wide at my intense
suggestion. She shakes Mehki and he jumps up looking like he is about
to kill someone.

"Get your clothes on! We have to go see what BJ wants." I announce
yet again as Ann crawls out from underneath the covers making my dick
stir in my pants. This isn't the time to get hard knowing my life can be
over in just a little bit of time.

I kiss her forehead and hand her the clothes she was wearing when
we brung her here last night and she quickly tosses them on, throwing

her hair up in a messy bun. Mehki takes the longest throwing on some jeans and a tshirt. I already quickly dressed and am putting on my shoes.

"Well let us go see what Blow Job wants," Mehki jokes, as he opens the door to the camper and steps outside. Ann follows him and I am last locking the door behind us.

Doom, dream, and uneasiness fills me as we make our way through the other campers. When we make it all the way to the back a huge gathering of thirty or forty workers are gathered around and BJ himself is standing with a microphone in his hand.

The tall, lean, long haired man looks like he stepped out of someone's nightmares, if Marylin Manson meets Jack Skellington were to have babies the result would be our fearless leader BJ Monroe. The name doesn't suit him at all, something like Damien or Dante would fit, but nope BJ is what he is called and I'm unsure of what BJ even means.

BJ's eyes cast out over the crew before he opens his mouth to speak. "Incase you didn't know Judd Parsons is missing. He hasn't been seen since he closed down his game last night. He probably got drunk and wandered off somewhere. If you see him let him know that we are looking for him. Also, I want to announce that Mayor Carpe has asked us to stay here in Jackson so we will be setting up the site for a more permanent residency. I'm sure some of you will decide to leave us and for that I truly understand, you can talk to me privately about it, if you wish to go. The rest of us however will be adding to the family with acts like they use to have in the old time ways of the carnival. We are going to be bigger and better than we have ever been before."

My eyes scan the crowd. A few faces appeared disappointed while others cheered and shouted. Ann takes a hold of my hand and brings it to her lips and kisses my knuckles while Mehki draws us both to use and envelopes in a hug. Mehki grabs Ann and throws her over his shoulder and smacks her ass.

"Let's go," he says walking toward the campers.

"Where are we going? Let me down!" she smacks his ass and laughs but Mehki just holds onto her tighter.

I follow them to Ann's trailer, he puts her back on her feet and smiles down at her. "Where's your key?"

Ann climbs the stairs and grabs a key hidden overtop of the camper and pulls it out and puts it into the door lock and opens the door, it hits with a bang. "Why did you want to come here?"

He climbs up into the camper and begins to grab items and a bag throwing items into it. "What the fuck do you think you are doing Mehki?"

"You're moving in with us, Hellion," he says as he picks up a bag of weed, looks it over and shoves it into his pocket.

"You're camper is too small for all three of us." She starts placing things out of the bag back onto the shelves. I stare at them my hands in my pockets and just smile. I can picture them fighting for dominance all the time and can't help but to feel how fun my life is going to be.

Ring around the Carousel- Ann

6 MONTHS LATER...

The guys wanted me to have BJ move me to the funhouse with them, but I had to put my foot down. They already forced me to move in with them. Okay, force is a little too strong of a word, but when Mehki started throwing my stuff into a bag, I didn't have much of a choice. Thankfully though, they have us moved into better mobile home on the carnival site, complete with plumbing, water, and electricity. I would call it a trailer park for freaks and carnies. It felt more like home to me, which is a foreign concept. I never felt like any place was home, but with my guy's by my side, I was home.

It is late when the final person in line leaves, which I'm grateful for. The juxtaposition of the music that plays over the speakers at the carousel are both spooky as hell and lively. It's enough to drive any person insane. I begin to clean up the litter that has been dropped and make sure that the ride is clean, when someone comes from behind me and grabs me.

"Just be quiet, don't say a word." the warmth of his breath in my ear is enough to feel heat rush to my pussy. I know who it is of course, it's my Pet, thinking he is in charge, yet once again. I'm going to have to show him that being a Dom is earned, not assumed, but for now I will play along.

His tongue glides the side of my neck before I feel his teeth sink into my flesh. I moan with desire as the carousel starts to turn. A flash of light catches my attention, I try to see what is making the light but all I see is black from head to toe. No face, just a humanoid shape coming towards me. Pet grabs me by my throat and pulls me back into him, his cock is hard and I can feel him through his pants. I wiggle my butt into him, causing him to growl in my ear. I don't need my bat to make him weak in the knees anymore.

Pet, in his disguise saunters before me, his hand whisks over my cheek. A glint in the night can be seen, my eyes adjust to the darkness as I see what he is holding. A knife. He skates hit down my chest, using it to pop off the buttons on my blouse. My shirt flies open exposing my bra, which he too cuts straight through the front of it. My breast on full display as he runs the blade down my sternum. There's a hitch in my breath as he glides the knife down, toward my shorts. Pup uses his free hand to help Pet push my shorts down past my knees. A gust of wind hits my bared skin causing it to pebble. I have no idea what to expect from them next, and without hesitancy, Pup kicks my legs open wider before dropping down to his knees. The hardness of the hilt of the knife as he runs it through my folds, has me trying to move, wishing he would just touch me, I need his touch, his mouth, him on me. I need relief of the build-up that the anticipation is causing. Once the knife is soaked with my wetness, he places the knife handle to by opening and pushes it into my cunt. Pet grasps my neck tighter and tighter, making it hard to breath, as Pup thrusts the knife into me, fucking me with it.

"You like that, don't you little, Hellion?" Pet's voice is harsh in my ear, coming out low and menacing.

His free hand cups my breast, as he uses his fingers to play with my hardening buds. God, I've never felt like this before so exposed. "You love being our fuck toy, letting us use you like we want." My core tightens at his words, he knows I love what they do to me.

Pup removes his mask, his blonde hair falling all around him before he takes my clit into his mouth, sucking, licking and nibbling my core he removes the knife and stands up. My pussy immediately wanting his mouth back on me. Pet releases his hold on my throat before he pushes me over the bench on the ride, my ass exposed, I hear the clanging of a belt before he shoves his cock inside me.

Pup is infront of me now working his own belt and I open my mouth wanting to taste him. My eyes flutter to his cock, his hand wrapped around as he pumps himself. I lick my lips as he climbs on the bench and he places himself just where he needs me before plunging his cock into the confines of my lips. With every thrust of Pet, I match my stride sucking Pup's cock, our noises filling the night air. Anyone could be watching, anyone can see what my guys are doing to me as the carousel circles around. I can hear the sounds of them kissing over me, the sounds of pleasure funneling to my ears and that makes me want them even more, driving me insane, needing them to make me come undone.

I use the edge of the wooden bench to hit my clit just right, I work myself as I am being fucked and in no time, I'm reaching my orgasm, tightening around Pet's cock, milking him. He reaches his own release spilling his jizz on my back and kissing me just when Pup explodes into my mouth, his cum escaping the sides of my mouth, he removes his cock with a loud pop as it leaves my lips. Pet stands up and helps me move my shorts back up, not wanting me to be exposed to anyone but them. *It's fine I guess that people know what we are doing, but they would be damned before letting someone actually see my body. Silly guys.*

Pup rights himself as well, he moves to me, his cum still on my lips, he takes his tongue and licks himself off me, then takes my lips with his. It's a deep hungary kiss that runs down to my toes. When he is finished he kisses my forehead and pulls away.

Jordan jumps off the ride and goes to the controls stopping it, so that Mehki can help me off. He takes off his shirt and hands it to me and I slip off my now ruined bra and blouse and slip his on.

"Let's go home, Hellion. You've had your fun for tonight." He slaps my ass before I run to Jordan who catches me and holds me to him.

The walk to our trailer isn't far, but fire hitting the darkened night catches my attention and I can't help but stop and stare. In between some trailers, a woman stands, pouring fluid from a bottle in her mouth a lit metal rod in her hand, fire forms the end of it and when she brings it to her mouth, she spits the fluid out of her mouth causing a scene that remind me of a dragon from folklore.

"She must be one of the new acts that BJ hired. A firebreather," I mutter, amused by the act before me. "She will be a hit." My eyes roam over the scene and hidden in the darkness, inconspicuous is BJ a look of bewilderment in his expression, his arms folded across his chest.

A smile covers my face as I take my guy's hands into mine. "Let's go home."

Home. I had always felt out of place, unwanted, never fitting in, but now among the ones that society deems unfit, crazy, weird or unusual is where I call home. A feeling of peace comes over me as we trudge toward our trailer and our slice of heaven among the freaks.

THE END.

If you like Mehki, Jordan, and Rogue's story you should check out Smoke & Mirrors. A gender-fluid love story featuring BJ, Inferno, and Seraphine. FTM romance.

Milton Keynes UK
Ingram Content Group UK Ltd.
UKHW011834120424
441050UK00001B/72